This activity book belongs to

____

MY FIRST DAY & MORE
ACTIVITY BOOK

My First Day of School & More Activity Book/Dr. Markethia Mull
Illustrations /Ochuko Eyaadah

Printed in the United States of America/Houston, TX

ISBN **979-8-9853160-6.3**

First Edition

Coloring Sheets

POPCORN
CHOCO BITS
Jellies
GUMMIES
MOVIE STAR
HAPPY & ME

Ealia
Ealia
Ealia

WELCOME TO
KINDERGARTEN

Ms Young
August 22 2022
SHAPES
A x2
Apple
L
Lion
E
Hen
I
Pig
O
Box

FORREST HILLS ELEMENTARY SCHOOL

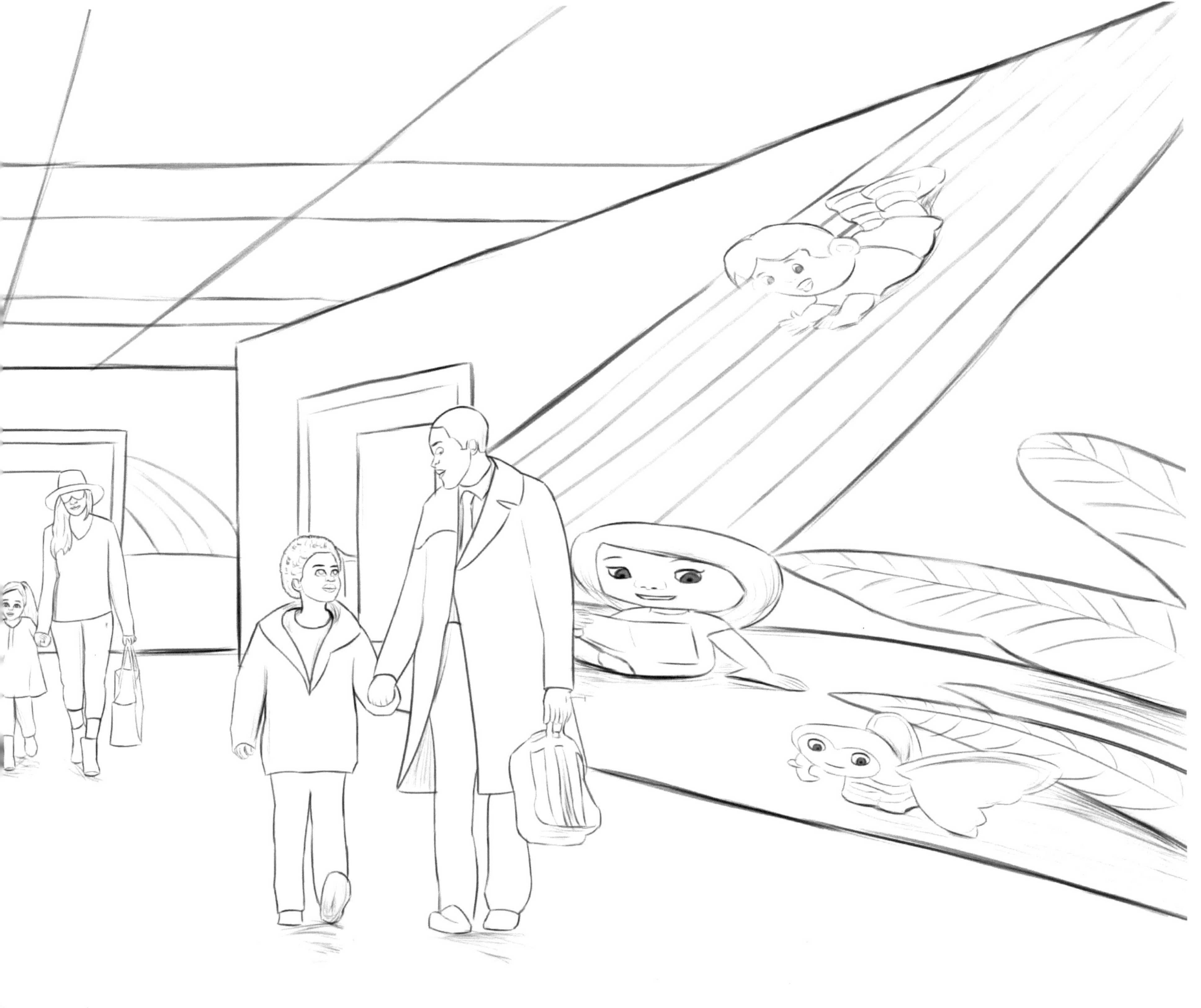

0 1 4 5
2 3 6 7

Let's Count!
1 2 3 4 5 6 7 8 9 10

A
B
C
a
b
c
NOW
AND
1. ALL
2. THE AL
3. READ AL

WING
TOO!
T US
ET SONG
MY FIRST
FLUTTERS
POP CORN
POP CORN

Reading and Math Activities

Comprehension Questions

1. Based on the title and picture, what is this book about? (before the read aloud)

2. What season or time of year does the story take place?

3. What was this story mostly or mainly about?

4. Based on the evidence from the text, why did Ealia have butterflies? How do you feel when you have butterflies?

5. What directions were Ealia given by her mother to dress for school?

6. What is a synonym for tummy?

7. Who is telling the story?

8. How did you feel coming to school? How did your mom or dad feel about you coming to school?

9. What can you conclude about Ealia, her mother, and the teacher?

Fill in the Blanks

My name is ________________________________.

Today is ________________________, ________________________ 20______.

This is my first day of school.

I am in the ______ grade.

I attend ________________________________ School.

My teacher's name is ________________________________.

My favorite thing about school is

________________________________.

Vocabulary Words

Direction: Use the words below to complete the crossword puzzle on the next page.

1. flutters

2. curious

3. imagine

4. fashion icon

5. peek

6. pretending

7. gulp

8. mural

9. greeting

10. nervous

11. butterflies

CROSSWORD PUZZLE

1. A condition of nervous or excitement.

2. Ask questions to find information or answers.

3. Mental image or picture in your mind.

4. A person who is known for fashion.

5. To look quickly at someone or something.

6. Acting or speaking to make appear to be true when it is not.

7. To swallow with a sound; to breathe in deeply.

8. Large painting or colorful art on a wall.

9. Polite words, gesture, or sign of welcome.

10. Showing or having a feeling of fear or worried.

11. Nervous feeling you get in your stomach.

First Day of School Activities

1. **Visualization to Make Inferences:** Read each cluster of sentences twice. Visualize an image from the sentences. Draw your pictures below and on the next page.

    A. I pick out my outfit for tomorrow. The first week of school is free dress week, then students have to wear uniforms. Those school uniforms are so plain. This first week I'm going to be a **fashion icon** (model) with my new shoes and hair accessories.

B. All the parents, including mine, leave when the teacher dismisses them. Ms. Young looks on as the parents exit the room. They all turn to wave goodbye to their kids. Mommy blows me a kiss, and Daddy smiles and gives a thumb up. I feel a little lump in my throat as I wave goodbye.

2. **Four Quadrants Summary:** Draw what happened at the beginning, middle, and end of the story. Have the students rename the story. Have students share their final product.

Title: ____

Beginning	Middle
End	Rename the Story

3.   **Figurative Language:** Complete the sentence using the words in the word bank.

a)   My backpack is <u>heavy</u> like an <u>elephant</u>.

b)   The ______________ is as tall as a ______________.

c)   The ______________ is quiet as a ______________.

d)   My teacher is ________ as a __________.

e)   My stomach is ________ like a ____________ in the sea.

f)   The boy filled a ____________ as he made tears like a ____________.

Word Bank:

princess	quiet	heavy	teacher	fish	flipping	tub
elephant	mouse	door	pretty	nervous	tree	rain shower

Word Search

My First Day of School

Backpack
Class
Elementary

Kindergarten
Lunchbox
Nervous

Newsletter
First Day
Greeting

Mural
Pretending
Peek

A	S	F	H	T	V	J	H	F	I	R	S	T	D	A	Y
N	W	Q	T	Y	U	I	O	C	H	Z	D	V	T	K	G
E	E	E	D	C	L	A	S	S	L	K	J	S	H	E	V
W	R	J	L	Y	U	D	G	Z	B	Q	E	E	F	C	M
S	F	C	V	B	X	F	W	R	T	Y	P	J	H	J	U
L	Z	B	Q	H	E	L	E	M	E	N	T	A	R	Y	R
E	K	N	M	L	S	X	Q	U	W	E	D	W	X	T	A
T	A	E	U	C	F	G	J	R	T	K	T	G	L	C	L
T	Z	H	B	A	C	K	P	A	C	K	R	I	W	X	I
E	C	V	B	N	M	H	Z	S	Q	E	T	Y	N	L	O
R	S	G	J	T	F	C	U	K	L	O	A	E	F	G	P
A	E	R	O	I	P	O	J	L	V	B	F	J	W	H	K
Q	F	C	N	F	V	R	T	L	U	N	C	H	B	O	X
Z	X	S	P	R	E	T	E	N	D	I	N	G	L	K	M
F	R	T	E	A	D	F	G	Q	W	R	L	V	C	X	N
K	I	N	D	E	R	G	A	R	T	E	N	G	J	T	V

Word Search

My First...

Book Cake Cell Phone Class
Food Game Job Meal
Shoes Thanksgiving Tooth Christmas

```
A C L A S S J H G L S V T J O C
X W E T Y U I O C H Z D V T K A
I E D L Q V Y S L K J S H C V K
O R J L L U D G T O O T H F C E
F F C V B P F W R T Y P J H J C
T Z B Q H U H S Z T A H L R Y K
U K N M L S X O U W I D W X T O
M E A L C F G J N T K C G L C L
N Z H E V U L X E E E K R G A M E
A T H A N K S G I V I N G N L O
F S G J T F C R K L O S H O E S
O E R O I P J J L V B F J W H K
O F J N F V R C H R I S T M A S
D X S O T E T E N D I N G L K M
F R T E B D F G Q W R L V C X N
E X G B D R V Q Z J L N B O O K
```

Word Search

Snacks

Apple   Banana   Yogurt   Oranges
Candy   Grapes   Donuts   Milk
Ice Cream   Popcorn   Pudding   Brownies

```
A S F H T V M H G L S V T J O S
X W Q T Y U I O C H Z D V T E G
I E D A P P L E L K J S H P V S
O R J L Y U K G Z B Q E A F C T
B R O W N I E S R T Y R J H J C
T Z B Q H U C S Z T G H L R Y K
D K N I C E C R E A M D W X T O
M O E U C F P J R T Y O G U R T
N Z N E V U L U E T K R B W X I
A C V U N M H Z D Q E T Y N L O
R S G J T F C R K D O A E F G R
C E R O I S J J L V I F J W H A
A F C N F V R T F Y K N I A E N
N X S P T B A N A N A D G L K G
D R T E A D F G Q W R L V C X E
Y X P O P C O R N J L N G J T S
```

Addition

Color the picture using the color code for the sum

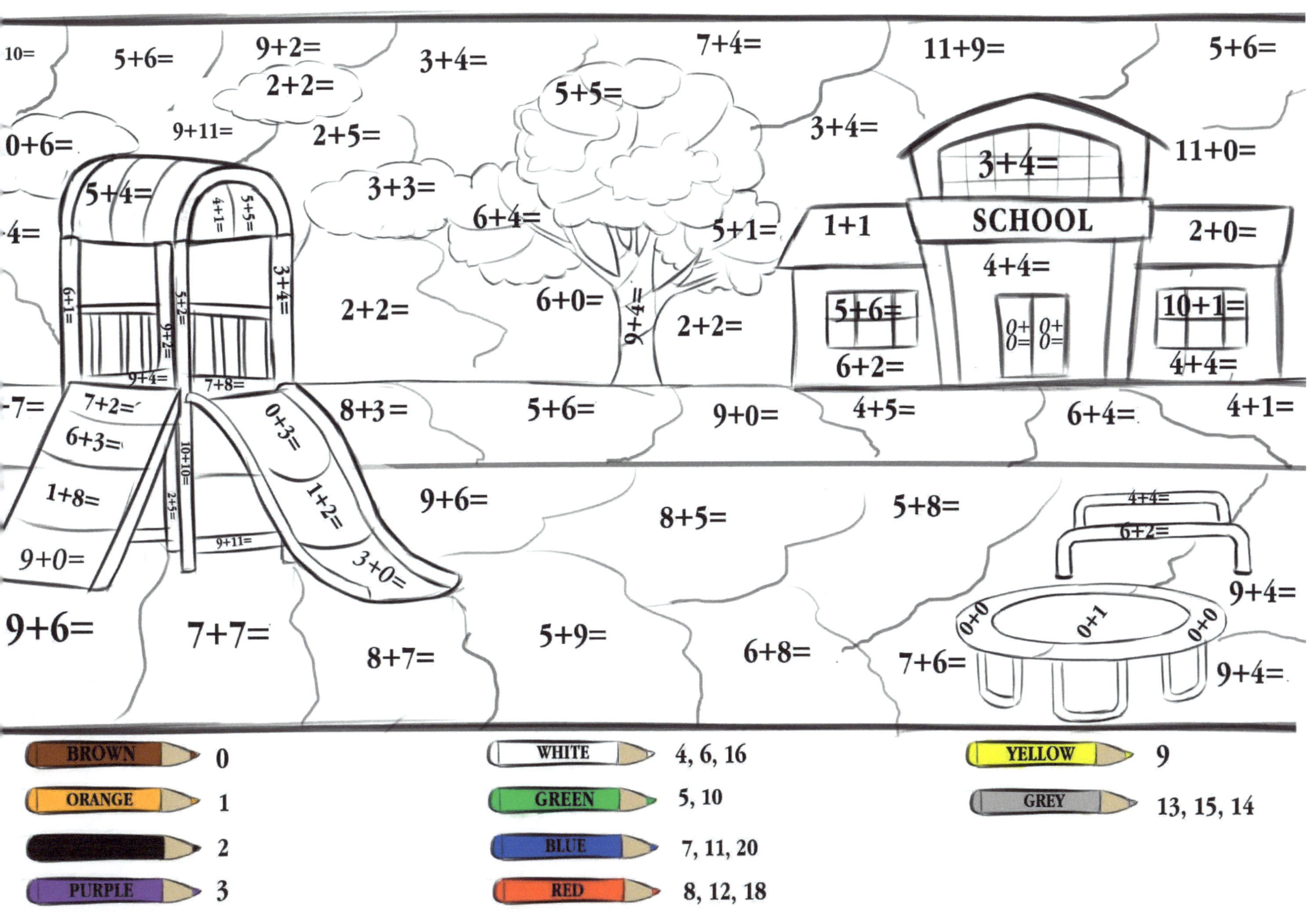

Color by Addition & Subtraction

Solve the problems with addition or subtraction. Use the color key code below to color the sum or difference.

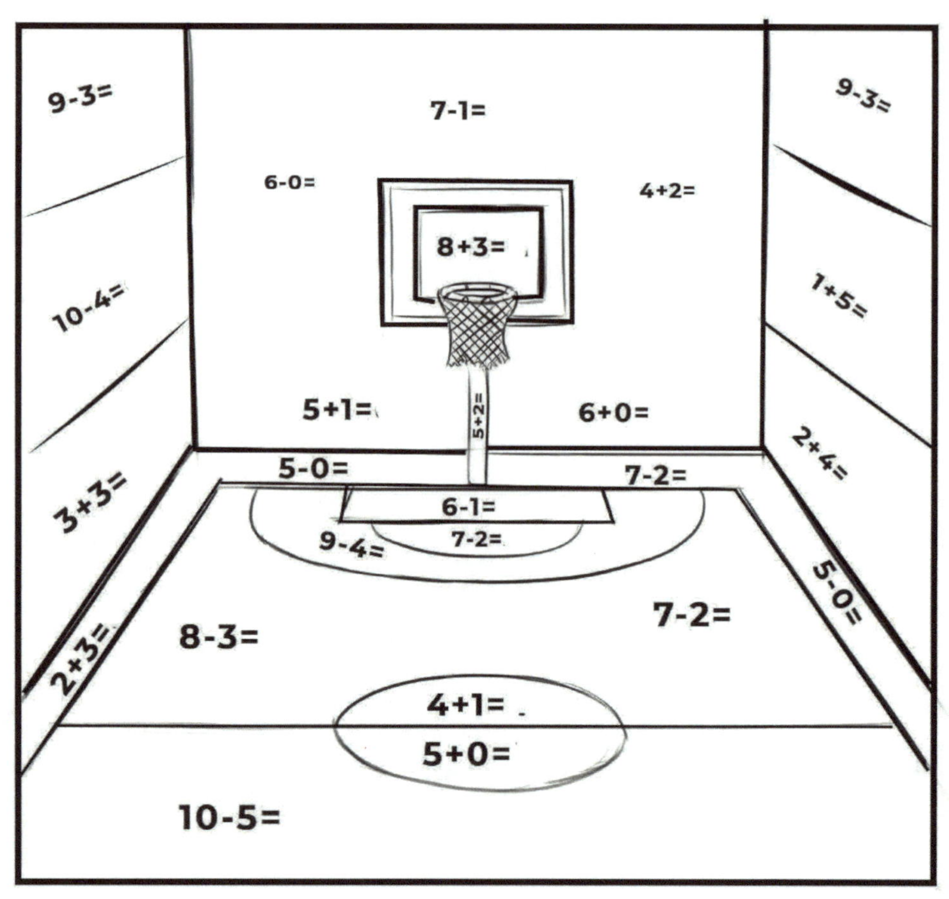

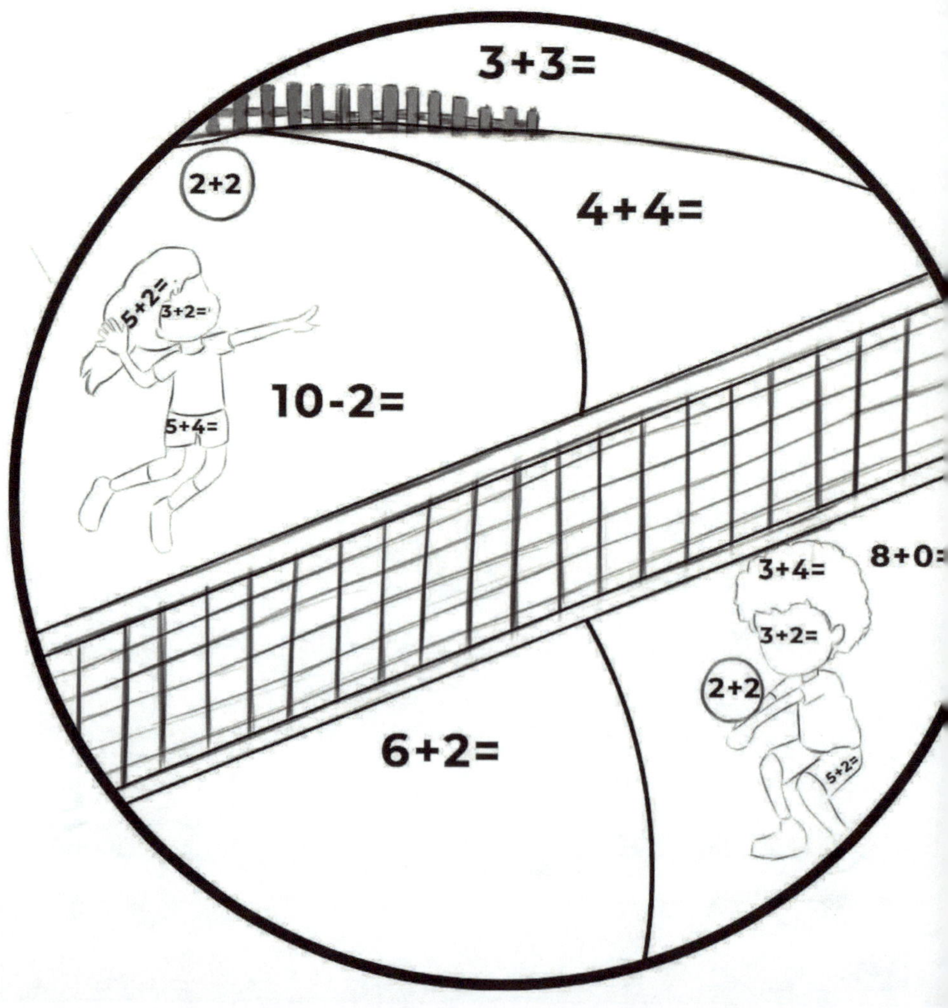

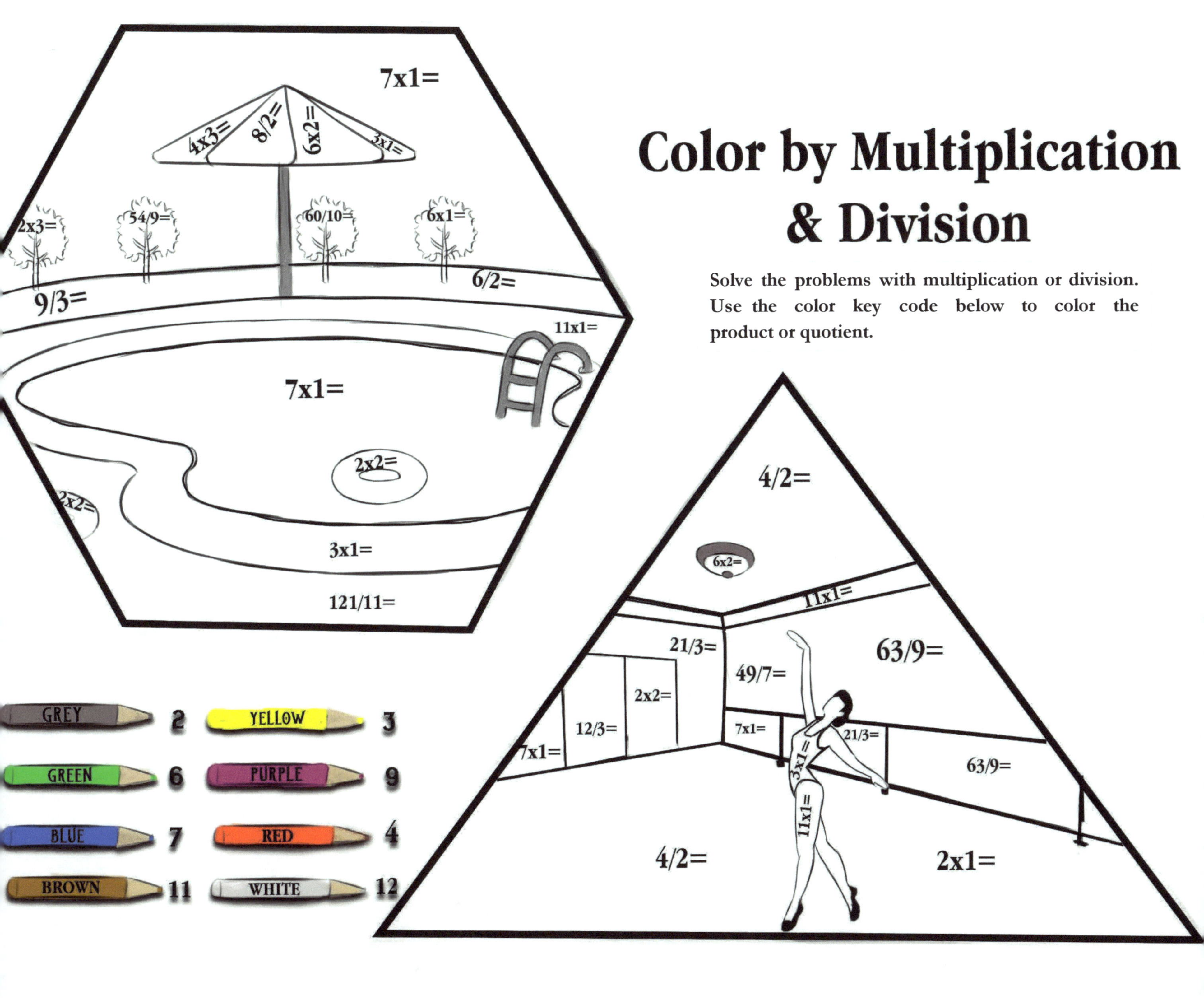

Color by Multiplication & Division
Solve the problems with multiplication or division. Use the color key code below to color the product or quotient.
7x1=
4x3=
8/2=
6x2=
3x1=
2x3=
54/9=
60/10=
6x1=
9/3=
6/2=
11x1=
7x1=
2x2=
2x2=
3x1=
121/11=
4/2=
6x2=
11x1=
21/3=
49/7=
63/9=
2x2=
12/3=
7x1=
21/3=
7x1=
3x1=
63/9=
11x1=
4/2=
2x1=
GREY   2   YELLOW   3
GREEN   6   PURPLE   9
BLUE   7   RED   4
BROWN   11   WHITE   12

* 9 7 9 8 9 8 5 3 1 6 0 6 3 *